Adios Cabron

Burn Sizzle Bleed Book II

James P. Johnson

Thank you, Leigh, Tommy, Reeshi, and Paul

For Jenny...

Adios Cabron

Thursday, December 30, 2021

Broomfield

Laura's naked with the covers over her head. Somewhere in the sheets, her phone buzzes.

...Nope, not today, Satan...

Laura ignores it.

The wind is whipping outside, the distant flow of the morning traffic reminding Laura of a creek during spring melt. Laura gathers the comforter closer.

...It's probably Katherine, checking on me...

When Laura woke up from an overdose last Thanksgiving, her mother was by her bed in the hospital.

"Get a job, find your feet.", her mother told her on the flight back from the Salt Lake City rehab. That was a month ago. Now, Laura's staying in her mother's condo.

...World finally matches how I feel...all it took

was a global pandemic...okay...

The nights are easy for Laura. She distracts herself; doom scrolling to the sound of network news, drinking her tea, and smoking her cigarettes. Eventually, Laura closes her eyes and another day is done. It's the mornings when Laura's head and body aches. Those are the worst.

...A pill, a bump, a shot, something...just to clear my head...

Laura fumbles to find something to focus on. This morning, she is trying to figure out how to get through the next few days.

...First New Year's Eve since rehab...

Laura's phone buzzes again as a blast of wind rattles the window frame. The blinds ripple and shake. Laura ignores her phone, again, as she throws off the covers.

...Can't keep lying to Katherine...

She examines her face and body in the bathroom mirror.

"Cheers."

This is Laura's chosen affirmation before another day of searching through minimum wage job postings. Laura would need three jobs to afford living in Denver.

It would break Laura's spirits, if she had any. She knows how to bullshit her way through an interview, but honesty and accountability are supposed to be important to her new sobriety.

...It's a lot easier if I'm high...

For now, Laura settles for the vicarious thrills of watching the world fall apart. The entertainment value is almost better than a bottomless mimosa.

Each day brings new levels of ecstatic pearl clutching, fragile egos, empty rage, and free-falling collapse. The phone delivers agonized wailing from anyone with thumbs.

...Here's a shot of misery...matter of fact, take one for each of the horsemen...

Every fifteen minutes, notifications ring out on her laptop.

...sip...

The television, oh the television. There's an unending waterfall of violence and death.

...So...Many...Bullets...

The dark electricity pouring out of all the screens wash over Laura and allow her to avoid her own mind.

It takes more than a dozen cigarettes, the

omnipresent screens, and about a gallon of green tea and honey to keep Laura from ordering delivery from the liquor store.

The wind roars while Laura leans against the kitchen counter and waits for the microwave to boil her mug of water. The phone rings again. The deluge of the day can be delayed but not ignored. Laura picks it up off the counter.

...It's Katherine, of course...

"Where are you?"

...Katherine likes to warm up before hurling this question...

The feverish edge in her mother's voice tells Laura this might not be the normal interrogation.

...She knows how to use Find Me... I guess Katherine deserves an answer...she did pay for rehab...

"I'm at the condo, mom"

"Turn on the news, my phone alert said there's a fire in Broomfield."

Laura smiles. Her mother moved to Florida years ago. Now she rolls around the community in her golf cart, chasing after former cops, soldiers, and firemen, living the life she missed as a single working mom.

...Katherine loves a uniform...

Laura imagines her mother scrolling through her phone, looking for Colorado news.

...Fire...not another school shooting...that's something new...and local too...tell me more...

Laura half listens to her mother give instructions to lock up the condo and go to her cousin's house in Denver. Laura walks into the living room and pulls open the curtains she usually keeps drawn all day.

...Too much sun...too much glare on all the screens...too easy to be distracted by the mountains...

The crisp blue Colorado sky is scarred by dark, roiling, smoke building in the middle distance. Laura holds her breath and feels her heart leap.

...Disaster...real, raging, human sorrow...and a little more than a mile down the road...

"Mom, I have to go."

Laura doesn't wait for a goodbye and hangs up. Standing naked in front of the living room window, Laura takes it all in. A huge black cloud of smoke and dust blots out most of the sky. There are sparks swirling in the wind.

Laura can see cars streaming eastbound on highway 36. Embers hover in the air above the big box stores on the other side of the highway. On her side of highway, a tree starts to glow with flame. Laura watches wisps of smoke rise from other trees.

Laura tells herself this is what she saw, and this is what she will tell anyone willing to listen.

Another blast of wind hits the building. Laura doesn't know if It's her body, or the building, that spasms.

The window rattles and Laura's stupor breaks. She shuts the curtains and starts picking up whatever is at hand.

...Laptop, power cord, oversized coffee cup, pack of cigarettes...

Laura dumps the pile on the rug at the front door and pulls her suitcase out of the hallway closet. Laura pulls on the sweater and sweatpants she left on the couch.

In the bedroom, Laura pulls open drawers and grabs handfuls of clothes, stuffing them into the suitcase. In the bathroom, she sweeps everything on the counter into a pillowcase. Laura wheels the suitcase to the front door, and stuffs everything in.

...There's a lot of room left...Another pass...

Laura takes a second to look around the condo. Her feet are cold against the vinyl flooring.

...Almost forgot to pee...

Laura returns to the hallway closet, pushes her feet into her Doc Martens, and pulls her coat off the hanger. Checking the pockets, Laura feels her keys, a lighter, and her knit cap with the ear flaps. This is her mother's idea of something kitschy to give to out of state visitors who are unprepared for surprise June storms, or sunny fall days turning cold when the sun goes down.

...Dozens of these in a storage unit somewhere...

Laura unlocks the apartment door, pulling the suitcase behind her. Her eyes scan the living room and kitchen for anything she's missed. She knows she's missing something. She closes the door, turns the key in the lock, and heads to the elevator.

...Too late now...

In the vestibule, a small crowd stands in front of the elevator looking down at their phones. Laura moves past them towards the stairwell. She yanks down on the fire alarm lever and pushes the door open.

...That'll get them moving...

Laura giggles as her suitcase bangs down the stairs behind her.

The garage is a mess. Smoke drifts in and is getting thicker. There's a line of cars standing still, honking at the car stuck in front of the closed gate. The fire alarm is ringing out and flashing. Laura gets in her car and closes her eyes. Her heart is pounding in her ears. There are sirens in the distance. A drop of sweat rolls down Laura's back and into the cleft of her ass.

Laura smiles. She has no idea 40 minutes have passed since she woke up. Laura can't visualize the roads she needs to drive to her cousin's house. Her mind is electrified, and one word keeps repeating in her head, in harmony with the alarms, horns, and sirens.

...Wheeee...

8th & Albion

Joe mutes the local news on the television and gets off the couch. He walks over to the living room window of his third story apartment, looking for the sunset.

...Still too light out...need to get a walk in anyway...

Joe pulls on his grey overcoat and walks down the stairs, exiting onto the alley. He looks up at the sky, buttons his coat, and sniffs the air for the familiar smell of smoke from big fires.

...Wind must have pushed it north...nothing but haze...not even a pretty sunset...it's almost anticlimactic...

Joe tries to ignore the ugliness as he walks through the alley. Next to the ramshackle fenced in patch of dirt his neighbors use as a dog run, there is a patio table, a small charcoal grill, and dumpsters.

...Ambitious, but someone failed...no chairs...just dog shit...

Joe listens to the clatter of activity from the open back door of the sushi restaurant across the alley.

...Good to see they're still open...

Joe crosses the street, walking past the new multiplex he's been waiting to open and the empty lot of dirt that's rumored to become a hotel.

...Might not happen now...

Across the street are the blocks of new apartments Joe watched go up over the last three years. Jenny calls the new buildings "the millennial kennels."

...Never not funny...

On the corner, Joe sees the legless man who's a fixture in the neighborhood slumped in his wheelchair.

Rose Hospital is a few blocks away, and the old VA hospital stands abandoned next to it. Joe has never been able to figure out where this guy lives, or what his name is. Joe thinks of him as The Wheelchair Man.

...Cold out...

Joe walks over to the man and bends down to look at his face. His eyes are closed. Joe taps him on the shoulder.

"Hey man, you okay?"

Wheelchair Man startles awake and squints one eye at Joe. The other eye is covered by the long stringy hair hanging over his face.

"Wha? Sure. Catchin' z's man."

"Do you need help?"

Wheelchair Man scrunches his face at Joe and waves a knotted hand at him.

"Nah."

Joe steps back and takes a second look.

...He's not old...not exactly young either...there's color in his cheeks, and his face and clothes look clean...can't be far from home...someone must be taking care of him...

"Alright, you sure? Don't stay out too long. It's going to be cold tonight."

Wheelchair Man shakes his head, and waves again. Joe turns and walks towards the hospital. Pulling his coat tighter, a joke from an old movie bubbles up in Joe's head.

...Damn shame, they threw away a perfectly good white boy...

The bells of the Catholic church down the road start ringing.

...No pots and pans anymore...now it's only church bells...I wonder how long that lasts...

Joe pulls out his phone and checks the time. Five. Jenny's probably on her way home from work. He unlocks his phone and stops himself before he dials her number.

...Keep circling back to Jenny...just text her...

"Dinner tonight?"

His phone buzzes in his hand before he can put it back in his pocket. Joe answers the call, and Jenny launches into a review of her day as she's driving home. Joe knows this is the prelude before she says she's tired and not up for company, so he listens and waits to talk about what's really on his mind.

"What about tomorrow? Are you going to be up for New Years?"

Three days, Joe has been pressing Jenny about New Year's Eve for three days.

...I need to stop...

"I don't know Joe."

Joe waits, listening for more. His silence is filled by the sound of her car moving down the highway.

...Somewhere on 6th Ave...almost home...

"Joe, I want to take a break."

"What do you mean?"

"I don't know."

"How long?"

"I don't know."

Joe hears her voice tighten with each answer.

In less than six months Joe has fallen in love with Jenny. Jenny often jokes Joe is her lockdown rebound.

...Too fast...too damn fast...she's been ready to move on for the last month...at least...

"What do you mean when you say take a break? Define it."

"Time alone, by myself."

"It would be easier if we broke up."

...Let's see if she takes the bait...

"Is this what you want?" Jenny's voice softens at this suggestion.

"No, I want to understand what you mean by taking a break."

They circle around like this a few more times.

Jenny evades and side steps, and Joe is stuck on repeat. It's a sickening rhythm.

...Keep asking the question...like some tired soap opera...you petulant baby...

"Okay, until when, for how long?"

"I don't know. Maybe we can still see each other a couple nights a week?"

"Like what we're doing now? If you want to see other people, say so. I don't have a problem with that."

...Accepting the smallest crumbs of her affection...so abject and craven...

"Let's see how New Years goes."

...A stay of execution...for the moment...already made the dinner reservation and put a down payment on the hotel room...I can get through work tomorrow...and dinner tomorrow night...after, I'll get good and drunk...face the consequences later...

Friday, December 31, 2021

Commerce City

Joe pulls his Subaru sedan into the warehouse parking lot and can see Howard. Full head of white hair, sturdy build and ruddy complexion, he stands inside the open warehouse garage bay doors with two fingers hooked through the handle of his blue enameled camping coffee mug.

...Kind of hard to miss...

Howard waits as the drivers and warehousemen gather for his end of year debrief. Howard is the V.P. and whenever he spends time in the warehouse, he likes to play up his hunter/outdoorsman persona.

...Thinks it makes him relatable...

A dozen people are shuffling into a semi-circle around Howard. Joe gives a wave as he pulls open the front door to the office. Howard raises his mug.

...Half of them are about to lose their jobs...

New Year's Eve is usually a slow day. The revenue for the year is already invoiced. Budgets, predictions, and plans have been submitted and reviewed. The only thing left is the approval from Howard.

...Should have been decided a month ago...

Climbing the stairs to the office, Joe can hear Bob singing along with the radio. It sounds like a bluesy, country fried guitar accompanied by a man's voice.

...Did he just rhyme blues, dues, and shoes...and say something about being dead...at least Bob's in harmony...

Joe walks in to see Bob sitting with his feet on the desk, cowboy boots crossed, cowboy hat on his knees. Bob reaches over to the radio on the windowsill and turns the volume down.

"Did you hear about the fire in Louisville?"

...A joke about the news media you hate so much...clever...why do you keep watching...

Bob stands, puts on his hat, and looks out of the window that has a view inside the warehouse. January is coming and Bob is excited to talk about going to the Stock Show, "Especially since we whupped that Chinese flu."

...Now you have an audience...here comes the rambling monologue...

Bob worked for the small food distribution company for over 20 years. As the other sales team leader, and the longest running employee, Bob is supposed to be training Joe to be his replacement. When Joe was hired, they spent three months in a van driving all over the Rocky Mountain West. The guys in the warehouse called them cabras montesas.

Joe learned all about Bob's ranch, Bob's two divorces, and the son who isn't talking to him. According to Bob, all of his time on the road is the reason why he's a 70 year old divorced dad. A year after he was hired, Joe learned the word cabron.

...Truth is, you're just an asshole...

Joe and Bob both spend 40 weeks a year traveling across nine states talking to grocery store managers and restaurant owners.

...Bound to happen when you spend way too much time alone...

Joe sits at his desk and nods. They're meeting with Howard this morning, and Joe is focused on reviewing his numbers one more time. Howard is the reason Joe took this job.

"You're a liberal arts refugee in a job with a spreadsheet bottom line. You understand people, and you can talk to anyone. I can teach you spreadsheets and databases, I can't teach people skills."

That was the speech Howard gave when he offered Joe the job. Since then, Howard helped Joe feel at home, especially since Joe is the only black person in the company. Joe listened to Howard's council, studied the software, and did what he was told. The company grew, and the numbers on the spreadsheet went from red, to green, to black.

...A lot has changed in the last two years...

Howard walks up the stairs and sits at the conference table on the other side of the room. Howard gestures for Joe and Bob come sit down. Bob tips his hat and starts down the stairs.

"I'll see you after lunch jefe?"

"Sure Bob."

Howard gives Bob a halfhearted wave, and watches Joe carry his open laptop over and sit down. Howard waits for Joe to get settled in and takes an extended moment of eye contact.

"Good morning."

...What a relief...Bob leaving means less interference, complaining, and bullshit...

"Good morning."

"I read your sales plan for next year. Good work."

"Thanks Howard."

"We think It's too optimistic."

...The numbers don't have emotions...you say that all the time...

"What?"

"You're a good leader, and the team has nothing but good things to say. It's easy to hit your numbers and keep the team happy when times are good. The next couple of years are going to be difficult. We're not confident you can hammer these guys into shape."

...The warehouse restructure makes sense now...it's not just reducing payroll...you wanted to make room to move me into another job title...

Joe listens to Howard explain it.

...Bottom line...you can't afford the cost of keeping two sales reps on the road. Especially when one of them won't retire as planned.

"Are you letting me go?"

...This is why Bob left...He knew this was coming...Son of a bitch...probably his plan...

"Joe, you're part of this family, and we think you can still make a contribution around here."

"What about my team?"

"Your team?" Howard shakes his head.

...You keep telling me there's a difference between taking ownership and being self-centered...thought that was some work/life balance bullshit...

"Bob is going to manage the drivers. You'll be responsible for the warehouse team."

...Not much of a choice...Take a pay cut and a demotion to a bullshit job...or quit...you won't have to pay me severance...

"When do you need an answer?"

"Later today. The new position starts on Monday. Take the rest of the day off, go home and think about it. I'll call you tonight."

12th & Eudora

Laura wakes up in her cousin's basement as the smell of toast, eggs, and coffee drift down from the kitchen upstairs. She reaches over for her phone and it's dead. Laura opens her mouth to yawn and a sound bursts from her, part laugh, part cry, part sigh.

...What the hell...

She rolls off the sofa bed and starts rummaging through her suitcase for her phone charger. The floorboards creak as her cousin Louanne walks to the basement door.

"You feeling hungry? I made breakfast.”

"In a minute.”

The concern in Louanne's voice makes Laura smile. Her mother's words echo in her head.

...That's why she's a great teacher...

Laura pulls on a hoodie and dumps her

suitcase out on the floor.

...Melatonin...dental floss...box of tampons...eyeliner...where's the fucking charger...

She's relieved when she sees the cord knotted in the pile.

When she gets upstairs, Laura mumbles monosyllabic responses to Louanne while she pours herself a coffee. Laura picks up a piece of toast and dips it in the coffee cup. Chewing the soggy toast, she looks at the eggs.

...I'm almost hungry enough to eat those...

"You used to like them scrambled, didn't you? Don't let them get cold."

Laura walks into the living room and flops down on the couch. She reaches over to plug her charger in an outlet.

"I'm meeting friends over at the Red Cross. They might need volunteers. You're welcome to join us if you're up to it."

Louanne looks over at Laura with a mixture of hope and curiosity.

"Uh huh." Laura grunts as she reaches for the remote on the coffee table.

She finds the local news. They're still talking

about the fire. It's under control. The chaos and mayhem have abated. A thousand homes were erased overnight.

...Miraculously, no one is dead...so far...

Louanne shuffles over and sits next to Laura on the couch. Laura makes room for her to sit down.

...She's trying to be a comfort...

The presence of another human being is something Laura hasn't experienced for a while.

...Don't fight it...

"Good morning."

"Good morning. It sounds like you have a frog in throat. I know a trick for that."

Last night they sat and watched the wall-to-wall live team coverage as burning fields glowed in the background. This morning, as the newscasters talk about healing and accountability, Laura listens to the sound of the kettle heating up and smells the sliced lemon in the air.

"Thank you again for letting me stay with you. It looks like my mom's condo is still standing. I'll probably go back tomorrow."

"Don't be silly. You've been through enough. Stay as long as you need to decompress."

Louanne walks back to the couch and bends to kiss Laura on the top of her head.

"Get some rest. And please, smoke outside, if you absolutely have to."

...So gentle and generous...

"I'll be back before dinner time. Maybe we can stay up and watch the ball drop?"

"Hmph."

Laura watches Louanne walk to the front door and pull on her puffy coat. Louanne picks up the box of canned food and swings the door shut behind herself with her foot.

...I want to judge her...It's too easy to see Louanne like the people on the news...performing...for a cookie...because they did the right thing...

Louanne's kindness is a simple matter of fact. She's going to help you, that's the way it is.

...You would be an asshole to say no, thank you...

The news anchors sound like they're also hungover after yesterday's flush of adrenaline.

...Felt more alive than since before

rehab...now there's only craving...and lurking boredom...this is the danger...

Laura struggles to mute the television, eventually turning it off.

...stupid remote...

Laura looks around the living room. It's neat and tidy, with framed family photos everywhere. There's a photo on a shelf of all the cousins up at Grand Lake from a long-ago summer.

Laura reaches over and picks it up. She finds herself in the front row, kneeling, with the rest of the youngest cousins. She's rolling her heavily lined eyes in reaction to something.

...I was, what, 12...

It was the summer Louanne came out. She brought a girlfriend with her and announced, "We're staying in this room."

...No one was surprised, and there was no debate...

Laura pulls on her vest and takes the framed photo outside with her. The shifting north wind carries the smell of stockyards in the air.

...Smells like Greeley...storm rolling in...

She lights a cigarette, thinking about that

summer. Louanne was in her early 20's, and the adults avoided the subject of her coming out. Louanne didn't need anyone to protect her, but Laura put the other kids on notice.

...Punched the first boy who joked under his breath...and told everyone I would do it again if they had something to say...

Back inside, Laura unplugs her phone and goes into the kitchen. She touches the kettle with the back of her hand. It's still warm.

...It's too quiet...

Laura peels the rind off and pops one of the lemon slices in her mouth. Chewing pulp, Laura throws her head back, mouth wide, and squeezes in honey. She chews some more, and swallows.

...pretty sure that's not what Louanne had in mind...same effect...

Laura pours herself another cup of coffee and considers the eggs again.

...need the protein, but it might be too late...hold on...

The lingering taste of honey on her tongue gives Laura an idea. She finds a jar of peanut butter and a knife, sets them down on the kitchen table with the remaining pieces of toast and her cup of coffee.

Laura pulls her phone from her hoodie pocket and starts scrolling through the dating app she's been lurking on for entertainment.

She starts swiping, and Joe's face pops up. Laura stops to stare at his photo.

...It began messy...sleeping with his best friend...but he belonged to me from the start...he would go whatever direction I pushed...and I pushed...

In his next photo, Joe is standing on a beach somewhere, drops of water reflecting from his bare brown chest. There's a ferris wheel in the distance behind him.

...Who took that one Joe...

In therapy, they told Laura that Joe was part of her self-destructive pattern.

...Not that simple...it was fun to see how far I could make him go...

Laura even tried to provoke him into hitting her. Joe stood up for himself.

...After that, he was defiant...

The next photo is Joe in a bar. Again, by himself, raising a drink towards the camera.

...His grin...so familiar...it might not have been

love...at least it felt like respect...couldn't trust it...everything was chaos and overwhelming...

Laura let Joe drift away and she moved on. She heard later that his friend Stevie died.

...Amazing I made it past 30...wreckage is all I have left...no one wants a grown-up relationship anymore...all apps and hook ups now...

Laura looks up from her phone and takes another look around Louanne's home; surrounded by all of the signposts of stability.

...Too late for me....

Laura hits the like button.

...Why not...he'll probably block me...

Laura opens her news feed and starts scrolling. Absent minded, Laura scoops peanut butter from the jar and eats it by the spoonful.

...Yummy...who knew...

8th & Albion

Joe sits at his kitchen table drinking coffee. He's spent most of the day job searching. All he can find is work from home, and essential worker postings.

...Shorthand for underpaid service labor...no future...or, there's the option to chauffeur people, or their food, around the city..

Joe downloads the apps and tries reading the terms and conditions. He stops and puts his phone down.

...Gig Worker...Sounds like more Essential Worker bullshit...

Joe stands up from the table and grabs his scarf and overcoat.

...a good walk might help...

Rush hour traffic on Colorado Blvd is heavy for a Friday. Joe wants to walk and think in peace, so he turns east on 8th Ave, drawn towards the ringing bells of the Catholic church.

...What if this is an opportunity instead of a rejection...

Joe sees Wheelchair Man just past the next intersection, huddled close to the apartment complex on the next block.

...It's tempting, freedom to choose your work hours, control your work environment...

The church bells stop ringing as Joe approaches Wheelchair Man. He has a cell phone plugged into an outlet on someone's porch.

"Looks like it's going to snow."

Wheelchair Man waves in the direction of the fading church bells, "Someone must be dead."

"What?"

"Or maybe, I'm dead drunk."

"Okay." Joe chuckles.

Wheelchair Man cackles wildly.

...Is he laughing at me...

Joe walks another block and looks back at Wheelchair man still laughing at his own joke. His feet start getting cold, so he turns North on Clermont and keeps walking.

...There but for the grace of God...

Joe pulls the brim of his baseball cap down against the wind in his face.

...What would you do with your time instead of working...spend all day in a coffee shop, writing...what a pipe dream...just because you like how a pen feels in your hand...shit don't make you a writer...

Joe walks past the abandoned VA Hospital, and the vacant, torn up lots left behind where the University of Colorado Hospital campus used to be.

...The 21st century is supposed to be a century of great black writers...read that online somewhere...has to be true...

The Millennial Kennels loom over the fenced in piles of overturned soil.

...Ridiculous...is there anything left to say after Morrison, Wright, Angelou, Baldwin, Ellison...

Joe turns back towards his apartment, crosses 8th into the alley behind his building, and unlocks the back door. He climbs the stairs to his apartment. He hangs his overcoat on the back of a chair and pours himself a cup from the dregs of the coffeepot. Joe pinches a little salt in the cup.

...How can anything I write sit on the same shelves...

He watches the cup spin in the microwave.

...But, what if...

The microwave dings.

Joe adds three teaspoons of sugar and stirs.

...Whatever's next, now is a good time for it...

His phone starts to buzz on the kitchen table. Joe puts the call on speaker, it's Howard.

"So, am I going to see you Monday?"

...What if...

"Joe?"

...Tell him something champ...

"Are you quitting on me Joe?"

"No, I'll be there."

Joe and Howard wish each other a Happy New Year and hang up.

...I have no intention of showing up to that job again... he's gonna have to fire me...a writer writes, a fighter fights...where did I read that...

12th & Eudora

Laura lays on the couch, resisting the urge to pick up the remote and turn on the television. She's worn out and beaten down by her own thoughts. All she wants is quiet. All this self-appraisal is new. A gift, and a curse, from rehab.

...Maybe a nap...

Louanne's house is a warm nest. Laura watches dust float in the sun shining through the windows. She stretches out, her hands resting on her neck and her belly. Laura's body relaxes into the pillowy couch. Still, she can't sleep.

...Could rub one out...might put me to sleep...

Instead, Laura picks up her phone and calls Roni to listen to her talk about her messy life. Roni knows all about the overdose and rehab. Laura is grateful when she answers, and the conversation quickly becomes a plan for New Year's Eve. "A quiet restaurant and some apps with the girls."

It's enough to get Laura off the couch and into the shower.

...Anything to not be here when Louanne gets home...oh god...the afterglow of selflessness she's gonna float in on...I can't handle it...

Laura puts together the best outfit she can from her pile of clothes on the basement floor and raiding Louanne's closet.

...Black mini dress...always works...some tights...and Docs...

There's a costume feather boa tucked away in the back of Louanne's closet. Laura wraps it over her shoulders and tries not to think too hard about where it's been, or why Louanne has it.

Laura is checking her make up for the third time when they arrive in a black SUV to pick her up.

...So exciting...

Larimer Square

Fat, heavy, flakes of snow are falling from the night sky when Laura, Roni, Trina, and Kate are dropped off at Larimer Square. They walk in unison down the blocked off street, their clicking heels muffled as the snow starts to dampen the pavement.

...I love this...the sound of our voices blending together...makes me feel strong...

The heavy snow obscures her vision as they walk to the restaurant, but Laura sees a man and a woman walking arm in arm toward them.

The pair are looking at each other and not paying attention to Laura and her friends. The women make room for the couple to walk through.

...What the hell...is that Joe...

Laura says Joe's name just low enough to register beneath her girlfriend's conversation, and he looks up.

...Guess he has a girlfriend...

Laura doesn't look back as the four women walk in the front door of the bar they used to hangout in before college.

...Denver is so small...

The hostess tells them their reservation is ready and walks them to their table. Men sitting with dates, and alone at the bar, watch them pass.

...Still got it...

Twenty years ago, fake IDs and easy cocaine were the thrill that brought them here. Now, feeling the eyes of half the restaurant follow them to their table is an instant rush that lifts Laura's mood.

...I shouldn't care, but right now, it's all I've got...it won't last forever...

When the server comes to the table for their drink order, Laura asks for a club soda with lemon while her girlfriends awkwardly struggle to decide. They eventually order club sodas. Except for Roni, she orders a virgin French 75.

"That's basically lemonade and soda." The

server informs Roni before she waves her away.

The other women at the table look at her.

"Roni, What the fuck?"

"What? I'm keeping it clean."

"It's an insult to the tradition."

...at least she's trying to have fun...

Her friends move on from giving Roni a hard time and settle into easy conversation, catching up with each other. Laura mostly listens.

The server brings their drinks, and Laura picks up Roni's drink to give it a taste.

Laura shrugs, "As long as you can live with yourself."

When the appetizers show up, everyone agrees how wonderful they are, and the mood at the table relaxes. Laura slips in and out of the conversation as Trina talks about her career, and Roni regales everyone with her adventures in dating.

They all quietly listen to Laura tell her story about escaping the fire, but they lean in when Kate opens up about struggling as a first-time mom during lockdown.

...How can I keep up with them...they're all doing something with their lives...I'm freeloading off my mom and trying not to die...again...

Champagne bottles start showing up at tables all around them, the server asks them how they would like to toast in the New Year.

Again, everyone hesitates. Before anyone can speak, Laura orders a round of French 75's for everyone.

"With Gin?"

"Fire away."

Her friends all stare at her. Trina is visibly irritated.

"What are you doing?"

"It's one drink. I can't let the tradition fall apart because of me."

Everyone at the table is silent.

"Seriously. I'll just have one, it'll be alright."

Larimer Square

Walking out of the restaurant, Joe puts his arm around Jenny. It's cold and starting to snow.

...Glad they're still in business...all the old places are going away...or changing beyond recognition...these new people have no knowledge or respect for the past...

Joe turns and looks at the big snowflakes landing on Jenny's cheeks and eyelashes. He takes a deep breath and lets it go.

...No one wants to hear it, champ...get over it...no one likes that guy...don't be that guy...

Jenny turns and looks into his eyes.

...Doesn't matter...when I'm with her, I'm the man I want to become...confident...capable of anything...

Paying attention to nothing else but each other, Joe and Jenny walk right through a group of women going in the other direction.

...Did someone say my name...

Joe looks up, but he can only see the backs of their heads as they walk through the falling snow towards the restaurant. Joe and Jenny walk back to the hotel.

...I wonder if she's up for some shenanigans...

"Let's try something new tonight."

"Like what?"

"Have you ever been tied up?"

"Not interested. That's giving up too much control."

"What if we have a safe word?"

"Why would I need a safe word?"

"To let me know how far to go, and when to stop."

"I can't just say stop, or slow down, or whatever?"

"That works too."

"What do you have in mind?"

"Let's explore, and see what we discover..."

Joe lets his unfinished sentence hang in the air.

...Her imagination is better than anything I

could conjure up…

Joe sees a photo booth in the hotel lobby next to the elevators.

"Want to take a picture?"

They sit in the booth and close the curtain. Jenny tries to brush the snow out of her hair as the machine clicks out a countdown. Joe puts his hands under her jaw, holding her face in his hands, and kisses her cheek. There's a flash and a click. They both turn smiling faces towards the camera. Flash, and a click. Jenny turns to kiss Joe deeply. Flash, click. The strip of photos fall out of the machine.

…We look so vulnerable…like teenagers…

Alone in the elevator, their hands push past the layers of coats and clothes as they kiss. Their body heat rises up between them. It feels like steam.

Moments after the door swings shut to their room, Jenny is bent over the edge of the bed, dress above her hips, and pantyhose down to her knees. Joe stands behind her, with his pants and his underwear stretched between his shins. Joe rubs himself on Jenny's wetness, teasing. She pushes back against Joe when he finally slides into her. Their rhythm becomes a steady pulse. Joe's head spins and dances. He reaches down to hold on to Jenny's hips. Mid stroke, he raises his hand and spanks her ass.

Jenny bucks him off, stands up, spins around with her fist cocked back, ready to punch him.

"What the fuck are you doing?"

"Just trying something new."

Joe can see the tears in her eyes, and he reaches out to embrace her.

"Don't."

Joe backs up to give her space. He can see she is enraged. He pulls his pants up and steps over their coats as he walks around the corner into the bathroom. He closes the door.

...What just happened...

He looks into his reflected eyes.

...Where did that come from...I wasn't trying to hurt her...I couldn't hurt her if I tried...whatever the real problem is, we should talk about it...

Joe walks out of the bathroom and finds Jenny sitting on the edge of the bed, sobbing. Joe freezes. As the New Year's celebration rises to crescendo outside, fireworks boom in the sky above Denver. The flashes create shadows and flares of light on the walls of the hotel room.

...This is not the New Year's I hoped for...

Saturday January 1, 2022

Larimer Square

As the fireworks over the 16th Street Mall finish, Roni raises her glass, "Real pain for my sham friends, champagne for my real friends."

The four women touch the rims of their champagne glasses to seal the toast. Roni announces to the table that she has a surprise.

"A car is picking us up in 15 minutes."

Outside, the snow is still falling. The flakes look heavy as they fly through the chill of the night air and land, weightless, on their skin, pausing before they melt.

A black SUV idles at the corner of 14th & Larimer, parking lights blinking. The women move quickly over the half block from the restaurant and climb in the car. Laura sits up front with the driver. The heat is blasting.

...Ooh, feels good...

The doors shut and they all excitedly shake off the cold. Laura turns to her friends in the second row, "Where are we going?"

Trina leans into Roni, "Yeah, what are you up to?"

Roni says nothing. Laura turns back around and buckles her seatbelt.

...so happy to be out of the cold...

The driver makes sure everyone is ready before he signals and pulls away from the curb. The SUV crawls slowly for six blocks and stops in front of the Convention Center. People dressed for a rave are walking in.

...Really...I can't remember the last time I went dancing...have I ever danced sober...

They're slow to get out of the SUV, trying to soak in all the warmth they can. The women can hear music echoing through the building as they hustle past the legs of the blue bear. Roni holds the door open and waves her friends inside.

"Do you guys remember Nathan?"

The women nervously glance at each other because Nathan was their drug dealer back in high school.

...He kept selling to me for years...stopped just

before the overdose...said he didn't want to watch me circle the drain...

"He got us VIP tickets tonight.

Laura, Kate, and Trina try to get their bearings as they follow Roni to the Will Call booth in the lobby.

...I want to dance...I'm craving it...the possibility didn't even occur to me...now, it's all I want to do...

20-year-olds dressed in thigh high boots and short shorts float past the three women. Bass notes thump through the convention center.

...Maybe Nathan forgot about his old friends...we'll all go hang out at Roni's condo...and that will be it...a quiet New Year reunion...

"Nathan came through again!"

Roni squeals, waving the VIP passes over her head. The women run to the entrance and are waved through the security screening.

When they walk into the main room the music is blasting. Most of the sparse crowd is pressed against the front of the stage where a DJ waves his hands above his head, conducting the pulsing throng. Large white balloons bounce over their heads.

Roni and Kate pick up the complimentary champagne as they walk past the ropes to the VIP section.

...This is not good...what excuse can I use to leave...it might take an hour to get a car in this weather...I only want to DANCE...

Nathan shows up holding what looks like a fancy cognac bottle in one hand and a barely dressed blonde in the other. She doesn't look like she should be drinking, but he pours liquor into her glass as she reaches into her dress and pulls money from her bra. Nathan leans down and whispers in her ear, sending her away with a swat on her half-covered ass.

Roni and Kate rush over and hug Nathan. Trina is standing next to Laura and pokes her with an elbow. Laura follows Trina's eyes and watches Nathan palm a small baggie of pills into Roni's hand.

...I've been on the receiving end of that sleight of hand more times than I can count...

Nathan waves at Laura, motioning for her and Trina to come over. Roni and Kate push him away. They come over and huddle in a circle with Laura and Trina. Roni flashes the pills and says something, but the music is too loud for Laura to hear.

...Escape is not going to be an option...

Roni raises her plastic champagne flute, howling, "To Nathan!"

...Please shut the fuck up about him...

Laura shouts over the music, "Can we just go dance?

Trina pulls Laura over to the silent disco room where everyone is wearing glowing headphones and dancing. It's quieter here. Laura and Trina show their VIP wristbands and are given free headphones.

The sound of far-off horns echo in counterpoint to the rhythm thumping in Laura's ears. An electronic flute lifts in a light melody and her body begins to bounce and sway.

Laura closes her eyes and lowers her head, shutting everything away.

...I'm practically homeless...no money...no hope...here I am anyway...

Laura's feet move from a shuffle to a step. Her shoulders shake to the staccato vocals. The beat drops away, and Laura's hips sway to the sound of the solo acoustic guitar.

...no one trusts me to do the right thing...my mother, my friends...no one...I don't blame them...I don't either...

The bass drops back in, the flute and the horns weave together in harmony, and sweat starts to break out on Laura's skin. She raises her hands to the sky and spins.

...fuck it...fuck them...fuck me...life is short...just let it flow...let...it...flow...

Laura claps her hands to the beat. She opens her eyes to make sure she doesn't bump into someone. She scans the people around her for Trina's face and can't find her. She turns another circle in the other direction and sees Nathan watching her from the edge of the crowd. She freezes. After a moment, she pulls the headphones from her ears and walks over to him.

"You having a good time?" His question hangs between them, sounding halfway like an offer.

Laura remembers the Rock God aura Nathan cultivated back in high school; black leather jacket draped over his lanky shoulders, torn t-shirt underneath, bony hips jutting over the top of ripped blue jeans. Laura scans the touch of gray around Nathan's temples, his Burberry plaid patterned sweater, the neat khakis, and his cream-colored canvas high tops.

...He's got a decent haircut now...looks like

someone's dad on vacation...or, fresh out of rehab...

"Trying to."

"I hear you're on the wagon these days. You look good. A lot better than the last time I saw you."

"I'm not surprised to see you still selling. It looks like you're moving up in the world. You could be a pimp."

"It's not like that. But, whatever. I'm glad to see you cleaned up. I was sure you weren't going to make it."

"I almost didn't."

"Thank goodness you made it out tonight. These girls need someone responsible to look out for them. They would be lost without you."

...We're fucked if that's true...

14th & Curtis

Joe sits in the loveseat, wrapped in the bed comforter, and listens to Jenny take a shower. The light of the cloudy sky leaks in around the edges of the drawn curtains.

...How did we get so sideways...

On their first date, Joe met Jenny one morning for coffee. She was dressed for the gym, yoga pants and a tank top under a zip up hoodie. Her profile said she was an athlete and she looked the part.

...Doesn't always mean it's the real thing...

They swapped lockdown stories; Jenny said she was impressed that Joe spent his summer getting fit, and she cried while talking about losing her job.

...the most genuine moment in my dating experience...I was sure I would never see her again...

Joe listens to the silence after the Jenny turns off the shower. The outside world no longer exists, and this moment is the only thing that matters to Joe. The bathroom door opens and Jenny walks out wearing only a towel wrapped around her hair.

...She's the real thing...no doubt...

Joe watches as she stands nude with her back to him, rummaging through her bag. Thicker in the hips and thighs, Jenny definitely has the body of someone who played sports in her youth and stays active as an adult.

...message received...take a long look...it's your last...no more for you...

"I need to move on Joe."

...Don't fight it, champ...

Jenny turns around and looks at him, putting on a sports bra and a matching pair of underwear.

"This isn't working for me anymore."

...Direct and focused...as always...the same way she handled our second date...

Joe was surprised when Jenny called him a few days after crying over her coffee. She asked what he was doing that weekend, and he asked her out for a second date. Jenny said yes to Indian food.

This time there were no tears. They talked about growing up in the 90's and why they like Denver. Jenny grew up in Wisconsin and enjoys Colorado's milder winters. Joe talked about how it used to be easier to live here. They kissed goodnight after he walked her to her car. As she pressed her body into his embrace, Joe ran his hands over Jenny's hips and pulled her closer.

...The chemistry was there at the start...

They are alone in the elevator ride down to the lobby. Jenny stands in the corner, close to the controls. Joe is against the wall on the other side. The space between them feels immeasurable.

...Thank God it's only three floors...

On their third date, Joe spent the night at her house. Sushi was delivered, rich people behaved badly on the television, while Joe and Jenny made out like teenagers on the couch. In the morning, they had sex again. Joe took his time, waiting for her wetness to cover his fingers before entering her. Jenny invited him to stay for coffee.

"This was nice", Jenny handed Joe a warm cup.

"Yes." Joe smiled at her, "We may have to do it again. Soon."

"Don't make yourself at home. Even if we have sex again, it doesn't mean this is a relationship."

Joe responded playfully, "If? You don't want a relationship?"

"Eventually. But I want something that will grow, not just dive right in."

Jenny stirred her coffee, watching Joe, "What do you want?"

"I guess I'd like someone who appreciates me. I don't know."

Joe felt like she was studying him as she sipped her coffee.

That was August. As Joe leans against the photo booth in the hotel lobby, he watches Jenny at the front desk. Joe pulls out his phone.

...Why am I even waiting for her...

Jenny walks across the lobby and opens her arms. As they embrace, Joe notices something in her hand.

"We can share a car."

"I already ordered one."

Jenny hands Joe the strip of photographs from the photo booth. He studies it as Jenny walks away.

...Man, this is not going to be easy...still, I respect she didn't drag it out...

Joe walks out to the car waiting for him on the corner. He checks in with the driver, tosses his backpack on the backseat, and slumps down next to it.

...single again...I'm tired of being treated like a widget...a fuckboi...

As the car quietly glides past the big blue bear at the convention center, Joe opens the dating app, searching for the settings to delete his profile. The notification bubble pops up.

"Joe, you have new likes!"

Instead, Joe scrolls through the archive of his past matches.

There was the childless international traveler. She called herself EastwickGal.

...Couldn't place her age, but the literary reference was probably more revealing than she intended...

She'd recently moved to Denver wanting to

see what it's all about. She was looking for a good place to retire. When they matched, she said it was because of how long Joe lived here.

...She showed up, and she put in some effort...her photos were a few years old, but I didn't care...one look was enough for me...the neckline on her blouse dipped well past her cleavage...and the flesh she showed off looked healthy and firm...I was just happy to be sharing company with a real live human being...

It didn't take long for Joe to understand she was a Trump voter.

...What she really wanted was an invite to the cookout...not that she would actually go...literally, or figuratively...the invite alone was the goal...and maybe being rewarded for simply showing up and looking pretty...that's supposed to erase any accusations of bigotry...I decided to test my theory...

"What's your favorite rap song?"

...This is usually all it takes to smoke out the impostors...and because I'm barely a shade darker than a brown paper bag, they assume I think like them...certain folks can't hide how repulsive they think Hip-Hop is...

The next day, she sent a text, "I can't see a

future together."

...Surprise, surprise, surprise...

Joe's next match went by Spacemama. Her profile said she was Hispanic, born and raised in Denver, and an accomplished engineer. She looked kind and soft in all the right places.

...Even described herself as...fluffy...

When they met, she looked like her photos, and everything about her was light and airy. A casual summer day on a brewery patio.

...She had no filter...She told wild stories about her college years on the east coast...we agreed that a reservoir is not a beach...she talked about how it felt to ship her only child off to college, and how she was enjoying her empty nest...She was up front about being in play time mode...

On their second date, they went to an arcade bar and played Centipede all night, trying to beat each other's high score.

He walked her to her car, and she asked, "How big is your cock?"

They slept with each other for a little over a month. They would see each other two, or three, days a week. Movies, dancing, hiking. All the things. Joe's wallet struggled to keep up.

Joe

He tried to switch things up, he invited her to hang out at his house and watch the Olympics. He cooked for her. She didn't say much when she walked into his apartment.

...It was easy to read her distaste when she looked around...she was constitutionally incapable of lying...she didn't have the skills...

Spacemama went silent on him for a few days. When he called to ask her out again, she told him, "We want different things."

A week later, Joe met Jenny for their coffee date.

...Time to get off this merry go round...at least take a break...

Joe hits the home button to find the settings again, and Laura's profile pops up. He sits up straight and scans her profile.

...There's no way that's really her...How is she still in Denver...This, I gotta see...

Joe taps the heart icon.

It's a Match!

15th & Central

...It could have been worse...

Laura waits in the lobby for the car to take her back to Louanne's house. The soft splash of traffic slicing through the snow on the highway below sets a rhythm to the quiet morning.

...Like water under the dock at Grand Lake...

Laura looks out at the city laid out on the other side of I-25. She can see the outline of the Flour Mill, the baseball stadium just beyond, and the whole other city that has sprouted in the space that was once a sprawling rail yard.

...what do they even call that neighborhood...this used to be the north side...now they call it The Highlands...Roni was lucky to buy a place early...or smart...she's always been both...no one could see what was coming...

The car pulls up, Laura tracks through the thin layer of fresh snow and sits in the back seat.

...I'm worn out...we managed to get to Roni's place without any damage...I'm sober...ish...I kept it to two drinks...everyone else got loaded...I had to baby sit them all night while they rolled...I managed say no...even when Roni offered me a bump to help get through the night...not counting what this car will cost, I managed to spend a little less than $100...

The car glides down 15th, a street where Laura spent a lot of her youth. She looks for the monuments of her past as she continues her self inventory.

...It was good to see everyone...it felt good to dance again...I've had worse nights...raves in the abandoned Flour Mill...all night sessions at Paris on the Platte...dancing at Rock Island...

Looking back, all Laura can see is the accumulation of nights, and memories that can't be erased.

...Nothing but ruins...failing out of community college...an abortion...and an overdose...how am I almost 40...

After her freshman year, Laura convinced her mom to finance a year of traveling instead of paying for another year of classes she wouldn't attend.

...I was wasting my time...and her money...

Laura spun the toy globe her dad left her, and her finger landed on Peru. She spent a month wandering Cusco before Tomas found her and took her in.

...Just in time, I was almost out of money...

Tomas was a young journalist from a family with money. He was sweet, but he was just as lost as Laura. They desperately clung to each other while trying to figure out their place in the world. That lasted three months. Laura left without warning.

...Did him a favor...saved both of us from a pair of golden handcuffs...

Laura doesn't notice the driver's smooth recovery as the car slips up the hill passing the Cash Register building on 17th, she is lost in her memories.

Laura moved to Colorado Springs and avoided Denver when she came back. It was close enough to home to feel safe, and far enough away she could stay hidden from her mother's prying and judgment. Laura waitressed and worked catering jobs.

...life started to feel fun...

That's how she met Brian. He was on his own as a wedding guest. Laura thought he was cute and pulled him into a coat closet. Brian was a Sargent in the Air Force and he spent that summer wooing Laura. Before long, she was pregnant, and he was about to be deployed. Brian didn't hesitate to propose.

...He didn't know it wasn't his...

Laura had slept with two other men that summer, and wasn't sure who the father was.

...I wasn't ready...

Laura wrote Brian a Dear John letter, got an abortion, and moved to Denver without looking back.

Laura looks for the bars and restaurants along 17th Avenue where she used to bartend. Even back then, it was a Denver she didn't recognize. The once sleepy cow town became a cultural and economic hub. Young people were moving here from all over the country and partying hard. Then Laura met Joe.

...Those days of reckless intensity still make no sense...it was easy to capture Joe's attention...and when I had it, I was the center of the universe...I couldn't get enough...it felt like stolen treasure...I didn't deserve it...I hated feeling that...

The first night, Laura looked Joe in the eyes and broke him down. She thought she was destroying him, striking a blow against misogyny. All she did was turn him on. Before Laura realized it, she was turned on too. The first night, Joe told her she was the only grown woman in a town full of little girls. It felt like the truth.

...By the time it was over, I was using...heavy...anything to avoid thinking...about everything...I started spiraling...that year turned into years of repeating the pattern...lost jobs...dead end relationships...feeling so alone...over and over...

Now, Laura just feels broken.

When COVID hit, it was a vacation Laura didn't know she needed. She didn't know what to do with herself. An old friend reopened their restaurant and asked her for help. The first chance she could go back to work felt like a second chance.

...I lied and told them I was sober...

It was the Friday after Thanksgiving.

...just finished a double shift...Katherine was in town from Florida...she could tell I was in trouble...

After close, she was doing rails with the kitchen staff out on the patio. Soon after, she was on her knees in the bathroom stall with the guy who gave her the coke. Later, they were hanging out with one of his friends. He handed Laura a piece of foil. As he held a flame under it, he told her it was hash. Laura was too wound up to go home and wanted to calm down. What she ended up smoking was heroin. Too much heroin.

When Laura opened her eyes in the hospital, her mother was standing there.

...It could have been worse...

Laura's phone vibrates with a notification. It's a text, from Joe.

...He's at The Thin Man...of course he is...he's going to be drinking...I can't...

Laura counts the three relationships of any real consequence in her life. One man wanted to take care of her, another, she almost married. She suspects Joe was the was one who actually loved her.

Laura looks up and sees the car is stopped at the light on Park Avenue. She tells the driver she's changing her destination.

"It's a bar, just down the road."

...Here he is all over again...at the place we met...where our dark chemistry first merged...Well, buddy, things have changed...Have you grown up...Are you strong enough...or, are you still a little boy playing at being a man...

Laura taps out a text in response.

"I'll be there in 5 min. You better be for real."

...It can't get any worse...

17th & Race

Joe dusts the snow off the picnic table on the back patio. He reclines on the bench, waiting for the bar to open. Despite the warm sun overhead, flurries drift down on Joe's upturned face. He pulls his overcoat tighter around himself.

...Not so bad...as long as you stay in the sun...

Troy opens the back door to the bar and rolls his eyes when he sees Joe.

"Boy, get out of the cold."

Joe holds the door as Troy carries a trash bag to the dumpster. Troy has been behind the bar at the Thin Man from day one. He and Joe are frequently the only black men in the building. Although neither will admit it, seeing each other in this place can be a small contentment. Sometimes he flirts with Joe, but Joe knows Troy is just working for his tip. Joe is flattered anyway. Troy is the only bartender Joe can share his personal life with. Once in a while, Troy shares some wisdom.

...like talking to a big brother...

Joe pulls up a stool at the bar. "Bourbon when you get a chance, please. I was dumped this morning."

Troy takes a moment to look at Joe. "You don't seem too devastated."

...He's right...I do feel...excited...freshly showered, and change of clothes...end of year bonus money in the bank...matching with Laura has got me...giddy...make no mistake, I need several drinks after last night...

Joe pulls out his phone. He searches through his contacts for Laura.

...Still in there...gotta mean something...

Joe taps out a text.

"Happy New Year. I saw we matched. Hit me up if you want to catch up. I'm at the Thin Man...trying to avoid a hangover. If this is still your number, you know who this is."

...Don't need to try too hard...the stakes are low... we already know what each other tastes like...we're way past the hard stuff...if it clicks, we'lll fall into the old rhythm...If not, no loss...anything to keep my mind off Jenny...

He scrolls through his texts with Jenny, trying to figure things out, maybe find a way to fix it. He stops at a nude Jenny sent him.

...Should probably delete it...

She sent it while he was on the road in West Texas, in response to his text telling her how much he missed her face. Even now, that text feels odd coming from him.

...Usually, it's out of sight, out of mind...but, whenever we were apart...I craved her...couldn't wait to hold her, smell her, taste her...

Troy places a glass in front of Joe and lifts a bottle of bourbon from the well. Joe looks up from his phone and gives him a nod.

Either Jenny understood how out of character this was for Joe and rewarded him with this photo, or she was just horny. It didn't matter. Joe cherishes it as a rare gift.

The pic shows Jenny lying in bed, wearing her blue silk robe. It's open, revealing one of her breasts, and half of the other. Joe's eyes follow the curve of her torso to her hip. One of her legs is propped open, revealing the soft patch of hair she started growing when Joe told her he liked, "a furry kitty."

She captioned the photo, "Are you sure It's my face you're missing?"

Regret blows through Joe.

...What the fuck do I need to do to get her back...

His mind twists down paths of plots and schemes, they're all dead ends.

...She's gone for good...a bad date with Laura is bound to be more fun than thinking about Jenny...anything to keep my mind off Jenny...

Joe throws back the bourbon, and it stops the plummeting sensation in his chest.

Temporarily.

Laura walks in, and Joe is struck right away how much she resembles Jenny.

...Jenny is more athletic, but they both have the same cheeks and nose...the same squared off chin...and the same look in the eyes...it's either a threat...or a laugh...

"Are you still drinking gin?"

Before Laura can answer or say hello, Joe orders a Gin Greyhound for her and a second bourbon for himself. Laura gestures to Troy indicating to go light on the gin. He nods, showing he understands. Mostly, It's a sign of recognition, a silent hello.

...You don't have a type, you have a pattern...read that somewhere...I don't think I have a type, but here's the evidence...If so, this is not going to go well...

"You're having both of those because I'm not drinking."

Joe shrugs

...Alright...just making a nice gesture...some appreciation would be nice...

"Still hung over from last night? Better off to keep drinking. It's working for me."

...He hasn't changed...still acting like a 20-year-old...How can a grown man live with no accountability...this might not go well...

"I was sad to hear about Stevie."

"Yeah," Joe slides his glass between his fingers. "He might have been the lucky one."

Laura changes the subject and tells her story of the last two days. Running away from the fire, staying with her cousin, the chaos of New Year's Eve, babysitting her friends. She considers asking Joe about his New Year's Eve, but he changes the subject and starts talking about the past, she lets it go.

As she listens to him, her eyes drift to just beneath the collar of his loose-fitting shirt. Laura can see the familiar space where she used to lay her head between Joe's neck and shoulder.

They sort through their time together and how things ended. Laura apologizes for fading out on him. Joe admits he was in love with Laura but was too much of a coward to do anything about it. Laura acknowledges that his courage might not have made a difference.

"I couldn't be reached."

...So much time has passed...his vulnerability is new...and he's so at ease...that same intense energy still flows between us...maybe one drink...

"Do they still have great artichoke dip here?"

Joe orders the dip, Laura picks up the drink sitting in front of Joe and drains what's left in the glass. The combination of sweet, tart, and the spicy gin loosens something in her shoulders a little.

"Let's have another round too."

Laura leans in to put down the glass, and Joe's eyes follow her hair to her shoulders and down her back to the curve of her ass rising off the barstool. Laura watches Joe's eyes roam over her body.

...still feels good...

Joe looks up and meets Laura's eyes.

...she caught me...good...

"Here's an idea, Let's go get a bottle and some groceries. Let me cook for you."

"Eating, drinking, and fucking. Always what we did best."

Joe reaches over and pulls Laura close. They kiss deeply.

8th & Albion

Joe is on the couch, alone. Naked under the comforter from his bed, he looks out his living room window at the clearing sky.

...Dusk, or dawn...how long did I sleep...

He listens to the flow of traffic on Colorado Boulevard.

...Sounds light...

Shedding the comforter, Joe pulls himself off the couch and walks into the kitchen. The apartment is warm, and the kitchen is a mess. A pack of room temperature chicken thighs and a bag of avocados are spilled open on the table. The cast iron is in the sink and sliced peppers are drying out on the cutting board. Joe shakes his head at the waste and starts cleaning up.

...I was raised better than this...

Standing at the sink washing dishes, the afternoon comes into focus. Joe was drunk by the time they walked into the grocery store. When he and Laura got to his apartment, they both had a grocery bag in each hand. He managed to mix up guacamole and make chips from fresh tortillas without causing any damage. He threw together black beans and the remnants of shredded cheese he found in the back of the fridge and called it nachos.

Laura sat at the table and watched, patiently listening to Joe talk about Jenny. While he cooked, Joe talked about how they met, and his other dating app adventures. Of course, he didn't tell Laura abut how heart sick he is and he only described New Year's Eve as "a bust."

Laura told Joe about her overdose, peppering her story with all sorts of clues, yet Joe has no idea about her time in rehab and her slowly disintegrating sobriety. Joe's only aware he caught her at the beginning of a bender. He's glad to be along for the ride.

Laura's phone kept buzzing the whole night, and to her credit she ignored every message and every call.

Joe watches the last of the water drain from the sink and remembers the group of women walking in Larimer Square.

...She must have seen me and Jenny last night...she had the grace to not say anything...or, she understood it would destroy the vibe...maybe she just doesn't care...

They ate nachos and drank red wine straight from the bottle while sitting on the living room floor. They kissed and pulled each other's clothes off, the taste of guacamole and cheese still in their mouths. Joe took his time. Being so close to Laura's body after so many years apart re-ignited him.

Joe finds his underwear on the floor and puts on his overcoat to carry the trash out. Joe reads the blue sky breaking through the clouds as a signal that it's going to get colder.

...I used to think of her body as an amusement park...time seems to have only improved my favorite parts of her...now, she's a lush garden...

Her nipples, as responsive as he remembers, hovered over his face. He reached up to kiss and suck on them. His hands gripped the familiar curve of her hips.

...Her ass will forever be fantastic...

Laura slid herself over his chest, stopping to perch on his chin. Joe looked up at her body, waiting to inhale her. Laura hesitated before lowering onto Joe's lips. She could feel him inching closer.

...He's eager...but gentle...deliberate...more sure...with his hands...lips...and tongue...the old darkness between us...it's still there...

Laura pinned his arms underneath her legs and could feel herself open over Joe's mouth. She pressed herself down onto him.

...He can handle it...he knows what I want...

Joe started sucking on Laura's clit. Laura leaned back to find his cock rising above his inner thigh. Joe focused his effort as Laura got wetter.

...Won't be satisfied until her juices are running down my cheeks...

Joe washes his hands and wipes the counter dry as he remembers inhaling the taste of her.

...never enough...

Joe maintained the pressure on her clit and started flicking his tongue.

...It's a special gift when she gives herself...better than most...

Leaning on the doorway of his bedroom, watching Laura, Joe is warmed by replaying the afternoon in his head.

...This is not how I imagined the day was going to go when I woke up this morning in the hotel with Jenny...

Joe's nightmare of New Year's Eve starts to soften and feel less painful.

...I'm a lucky boy...It's almost impossible, yet here she is...the right woman, in the right moment...I won't let her disappear from my life a second time...

Somewhere in the sheets, Laura's phone buzzes.

Laura is awake, sheets pulled over her head. She feels around for her phone. She finds one of her earrings before her hand grazes the vibrating metal and glass.

...can't keep ignoring it...It's Louanne...probably wondering where I am...it's been more than 24 hours...

Laura dismisses the call and sends a text, "I'm fine."

She hesitates, then drops a pin on her location.

...not sure if that comforts her or me...

"I have eggs if you're hungry."

Startled, Laura pokes her head out of the covers. She heard Joe banging around in the kitchen, but now he's leaning against the bedroom door.

...Something breaks open whenever he looks at me...but I keep second guessing things...

Laura sits up, looking at Joe, reading him while she puts her earring in. She examines his forearms, scans his chest, inspects his lips, deciphers his eyes.

...Those underwear are coming off...again...

Laura opens her mouth to speak, her voice echoing the words in her head.

"I think you should fuck me."

Joe steps to the side of the bed. He pulls the sheet away, revealing Laura's body. Laura doesn't move to cover herself. She lets Joe take a long look in the fading light of the setting sun. He lays down in the bed next to her and reaches his fingers into her hair. Joe pulls her body closer to him.

Laura opens her mouth, accepting his tongue with warmth and wetness, exciting Joe. She reaches down, feeling Joe throb and pulse in her hand. Laura pulls her head away from Joe's grasp and slowly begins a trail of kisses over his neck, across his chest, and down to his navel.

...I want to feel him grow in my mouth...

He's already half erect as she wets her lips so the head of his cock can slide over her tongue.

...No matter what time of day it is, there's no better way to wake up...her mouth is the center of the universe...

He tries to watch her, but her hair keeps falling over her face. Joe reaches down to move her hair, but she smacks his hand away. Laura moves her hand up and over Joe's cock slowly and starts again.

...Let's have some fun...it's been too long...

The combination of Laura's enthusiasm and her slow approach drives Joe to his edge.

...Her control is agonizing...I want to see her mouth covering me...watch her cheeks draw in...

Joe reaches down again to move her hair, and this time Laura grabs Joe's wrist and puts his hand behind his head. She picks up his other hand from his chest and moves it behind his head.

Laura takes his chin in her hand and moves her face close to his. Neither of them blink.

...I submit...whatever you demand...

Laura can feel Joe, still firm in her other hand, his body quivers beneath her. His silent yearning and her command are known and unspoken.

...I own him...he needs this...

Laura swings her leg over and reverse straddles Joe.

... Okay, here you go...you love this ass...

She rubs her folds against him, covering him with her slickness.

...enough teasing...

Laura guides Joe inside her and lets him do the

rest. Laura grinds against Joe's as she watches the sky change from pink, to gold, to indigo.

When Laura gets out of the shower, Joe has already left to pick up sushi. Laura pulls on a pair of Joe's boxers and one of his hoodies.

She sits on the couch, scrolling through her messages. Roni says thanks for baby sitting them, the others are checking that she's safe. There's a dozen messages from Louanne. Laura calls her and says she's okay.

"Are you?"

...Loaded question...she's too polite to straight up ask if I'm still sober...mind your own business...

"Am I far from your house?"

"You're practically in my neighborhood. Do you need me to come get you? It's a short walk. I can be there in five minutes."

"No. I'll call you in the morning."

Joe walks in with the food and four small bottles of sake as Laura ends the call.

"Go ahead and start without me, I'm going to jump in the shower real quick."

Laura twists the cap open on one of the little blue bottles and throws it back. It's strong, burning the back of her throat.

Smelling like soap and wearing the matching

sweatpants to the hoodie that Laura pulled out of his closet, Joe sits next to Laura on the couch. They curl up together and scarf down the sushi rolls, drinking the rest of the sake.

While they eat, Joe turns on the television and starts a show.

"This is cool as fuck. Have you seen it?"

...Another square middle class white guy getting mixed up with swarthy drug dealers from south of the border...it's never pills, powder, and alcohol...It's always meth...

Joe's hands wander over Laura's hip and slide under the boxers she stole from his dresser. Encouraged by his fingers, it only takes a nudge from Laura's hips to distract him from the television.

...Come and get it...

She keeps her ass in the air, letting him take control behind her. Joe drives her face into the couch cushions. Laura can smell his sweat in the woven fabric.

...Take it...take me...

After, Joe collapses next to Laura and stretches out his leg to rub his foot against hers.

Laura jumps up, "Let's go out and see the stars."

They dress; Joe changes into long underwear and jeans, Laura puts on the sweatpants Joe was wearing, tucking them into her untied Doc Martens.

Joe watches Laura check herself in the mirror on the back of his bedroom door and can see the points of her nipples beneath the fabric of the hoodie.

...cute...

Sitting in his car, Joe asks as she plugs her phone into the charger, "North, South, East, or West?"

This is his personal ritual for going on a pleasure drive. He's never shared it with anyone. Laura just points without looking up from her phone. He doesn't know if she means to point West, but that's the direction he drives.

Laura asks if they can get to the nearest dispensary before it closes.

"You know I don't smoke."

"That's okay. We'll get gummies."

The night sky is clear and black as Joe points his car West on Highway 6. The radio plays quietly and the car is warm. The snow is cleared from the road and there's no traffic.

The flashing lights of the radio towers on Lookout Mountain draw Joe's attention. Laura looks out the passenger window.

...the food, the sake...the whole vibe...I needed this...

The Subaru does a slow climb up the tight switchbacks. It's late. They have the view of the entire city to themselves. Joe pulls into a parking spot and realizes the edible is kicking in.

Sunday, January 2, 2022

Lookout Mountain

The lights of the city glitter in the distance, like stars on a dark lake. To the north, there is a pool of glowing arc lights, where rescue and recovery teams are gathered.

...Head feels mushy...the lights, the sky...feels like floating...not uncomfortable...unsteady...

Joe reaches across to Laura and his hand sinks into her lap. She reaches over and pulls his face to hers. Their lips find each other. Joe slides his hand between her thighs. Laura grasps Joe by the wrist and pushes his hand inside the waistband of the sweats. She raises her hips to meet his fingertips. Moving them in a slow circle, Joe matches her pressure.

...he's eager for direction...

Joe buries his head in Laura's neck, kissing her collarbone.

...she smells like grapes...not sugary sweet...not sharp like wine either...reminds me of the grapevines in my mother's backyard...

Joe listens for the sound of Laura's breathing. Her body is rigid, like she's holding her breath.

...she's not here with me...maybe she's just high...

Joe sits back in the driver's seat.

...Oh my god, the lights...

Without thinking, the words fall out of him. "I know you're going through some shit right now. So am I."

Laura lets his words hang in the air, feeling no need to respond.

...Where is this going...

"I haven't felt this good in a long time. Not since the last time we were together, really. I don't want it to go away. Not like last time."

Laura closes her eyes.

...Here come the storm clouds...everything's so heavy with him...it can't just be fun...

"Anything can happen, right, but in the next five years, if we're both still single, we could make this something real."

...Is this his idea of a proposal... I'm too high

for this half assed shit...

Instead of saying any of this, Laura decides to fuck with him.

"Why wait? Let's go for it now?"

Joe tries to hide his excitement.

"Quit fucking with me. We're both too fucked up."

...He has no idea...

She takes his hand in hers. Let's just watch the lights and the stars."

Laura's already done more thinking about herself in the last 24 hours than the month since she left rehab.

...I can't get out of my head...I don't want to think about anything...anymore...

Laura picks up her phone. There are a bunch of messages from her girlfriends. They want her to come out and play, and Nathan is with them.

...That'll put the wind in my sails...

"They're at some bar in Globeville."

"Sure, why not." Joe backs the car onto the road, pointing it downhill. Flush with adrenaline, his head feels clear, but he goes slow anyway.

At the bottom of the hill, Joe turns onto Highway 6.

...Straight, wide open road...let's go...

Joe pulls a CD out of the visor and slides it into the slot in the dashboard.

"Let's see if we can get there before last call. Hold on to something."

He clicks the skip button a few times to find the song he wants. An air horn blasts from the car speakers followed by an army of drums. Joe mashes the accelerator and feels the six cylinders respond with vigor.

Laura looks over at the speedometer as it slides past 90. She looks at Joe.

...Didn't know he had it in him...

The car does a small hop into the air as it crests the hill just before Union Blvd. Joe watches the needle creep towards the 100 mph mark. He's never driven this fast before.

...I need this...just to calm down...

45th & Grant

The bar is nearly empty.

A little white dog keeping watch under a table in the corner raises her head when Joe and Laura walk in. Joe stops to get his bearings and reads the room.

...Seems cozy...

A mirror hangs on the full length of the wall opposite the front door. There's a bar along the left side of the room. Next to the bar, a small window opens into a kitchen. The sign hanging above it says Order Here. There are reupholstered couches and wicker chairs throughout the room. Two or three of them are replicas of the wicker throne Huey Newton sat on in the famous photograph from the 60's. Old rugs cover the concrete floors.

...Somebody got a lot of furniture after granny died...

Tucked into a corner of the Mousetrap and a stone's throw from the Stock Show Complex, this used to be a working-class Hispanic neighborhood.

...Globeville...the last frontier of gentrification...spillover from the Millennial Kennels on Brighton Blvd...and a launch pad for house flippers into Elyria-Swansea...

The woman behind the bar yells out last call, prompting Laura to walk over to the bar. Joe wanders to the kitchen window. He's got the munchies.

A small easel holds a placard in the window with five menu items listed, including a choice of sides and sauces. On the other side of the window, the kitchen looks empty.

...Reads like a bastardized Thai, or Chinese, menu...probably calling it fusion...

Joe overhears Laura ask for two French 75's as he walks over to the bar. Laura pays for the drinks and asks for directions to the patio. The bartender points to the door next to the bar.

Joe follows Laura through the doorway and down two steps. They walk past the kitchen and stairs that go down to a basement and turn into a small room with more floral upholstered furniture. An explosion of laughter comes through the archway opening onto a larger room with chairs, tables, and an elevated stage.

There's garland strung on the ceiling between light fixtures that are shaped like clouds. Rugs, funky wallpaper, painted brick, and potted plants with lights strung in them fill out the room. In the center, a disco ball hangs from the ceiling.

Joe vaguely recognizes Laura's friends as they get up to hug her. He's seen some of them in other places around town. They politely greet him and return to listening intently to Nathan, the only other man in the room.

Nathan is sitting in one of the replica wicker thrones, holding court, "Anyway, it was 1983 and Hip hop was everywhere on the North side"

He describes what it was like to be bussed to North High School and starts dropping artist names from early hip hop that he used to listen to.

...Okay, Columbus...

Joe looks around the room and feels a flash of heat in his neck and shoulders. Of the eight people in the room, he's the only Black man.

...Once again...

Joe's heart thuds in his ears and his armpits start to sweat. He excuses himself and walks back to the bar with his drink.

"Can I get one of these with Bourbon instead?"

Joe closes his eyes, turning his attention inward to relax. A low vibration hums through him.

...freight train engines a few blocks away...

The bartender returns, presenting a rocks glass, champagne fizzing up to a sugar-coated rim. Joe takes a deep sip of the sweet, bitter, bubbly drink.

...I have to get out of this town...

45th & Grant

Laura huddles with her friends, smoking a cigarette while they wait for their car to arrive. **They surround her** with questions.

"Are you okay?"

"Is he still any good in bed?"

"Sure you don't want a ride?"

"Is he being good to you?"

...They can't help themselves...they really are trying...

"We're just having fun. Yeah, he's being good. I'll be okay. I'll tell you all about it tomorrow."

...Wish I was being good to myself...can we all just go back to lock down...

They each hug Laura when their car pulls up. Laura walks towards Joe's car and sees Nathan point in her direction as he talks to Joe.

...Clean up on aisle 10...

The two girls hanging out with Nathan stand shivering on the sidewalk.

"Dude, can we get a ride? It's too cold to keep waiting for this stupid car!"

"C'mon."

Joe unlocks his car with the remote and they all pile in. Joe starts the car and turns the heat up all the way.

Everyone is quiet except for the sound of Nathan and the girls rubbing their hands and stomping their feet.

Nathan breaks the silence, waving a baggie of pills, "Who wants to keep partying?"

Joe offers for everyone to come back to his place. Laura is relived. The idea of being sober and alone with Joe makes her itchy.

8th & Albion

Joe offers everything he has, beer, whiskey, wine, as soon as they walk in. Before he can start mixing drinks, Nathan starts handing out small tablets of "left over Molly from New Years."

Laura doesn't hesitate, grabbing two pills, handing one to Joe as she walks through the living room and into Joe's bedroom.

...Maybe he'll loosen up...

Nathan stands in front of a bookshelf and asks, "Did you read all of these?"

Joe ignores the barbed edge in Nathan's question as he follows Laura into the bedroom and closes the door behind him.

"Are you sure you want to do this?"

"Yes, let's have some fun!""

"Why didn't you tell me you just got out of

rehab?"

"Look, I'm okay. Can we just keep things casual?"

Joe starts pacing the room.

"Casual? Is that all you want?"

"Yes, that's all I want, and I don't owe you anything else."

Joe stops and looks at Laura.

"Fucking white girls."

"Why does it have to be about that?"

"Y'all only want this dick because you can't handle the human being attached to it. I'm not some kind of walking dildo."

"That's not fair. Like you said, I have my own stuff I'm dealing with."

"If you were able to see me as a person, it might occur to you I could help you. Instead, the only thing I'm good for is some freaky fucking. I'm disposable."

Laura laughs, sitting up on the bed.

"Grow up. I'm trying to save my own life. I don't need you to take care of me."

...This has got to stop...

"What do you have to offer besides a generous

fuck? You're empty, yearning for someone to tell you who to be. You're barely an adult."

Laura stands up and opens the bedroom door.

"You really know how to ruin a good time."

Nathan and his girls are curled up in a pile of couch cushions and pillows on the living room floor when Laura walks out of the bedroom. She turns the corner into the kitchen, picking up a bottle of wine. She can hear Joe grab his coat and slam the door as he leaves the apartment.

...I was right about you from the start...figure your own shit out...I can't help you baby boy...

8th & Colorado Blvd

...Fucking white girls...who needs it...

Joe stands on the corner holding a hot cup of convenience store coffee. He pulls the molly tab out of his pocket and looks at it for a second before tossing it in his mouth and sipping coffee to help him swallow. It tastes awful.

...It's been a few years, but...fuck it...

Joe crosses Colorado Boulevard, taking another swig of coffee before tossing the cup in the trash can at the bus stop. He walks another block, buttoning his coat and tying his scarf around his neck before turning North into the Congress Park neighborhood.

...What was that about...your drug dealer friend told me about you getting out of rehab...

Joe looks up and sees the elementary school playground. He walks over, sits on one of the swings, and looks up at the night sky.

...Fuck this shitty place and all the shitty people...I used to know Denver...not any more...

The sky is clear and the stars seem to flash and sparkle.

...Probably just satellite...it doesn't matter...

Joe feels his body warming in his coat. For the second time tonight, his heart feels like it will fly out of his chest.

...Oh man...oh...I'm starting to roll...

Joe wants to get up and start moving, feel the night air against his skin. He wants to move his body. Everything is in slow motion, like moving through honey.

...Need to get back inside...sweat feels so good...I'll probably freeze to death if I don't keep moving...

On the other side of Colorado Blvd, Joe walks down Hale Parkway. It looks like there's a pile of clothes on the sidewalk ahead of him. Joe stops on the corner before turn towards his apartment.

The pile of clothes looks like it's moving, and

Joe thinks he can see a pale white foot.

...I'm not supposed to be seeing shit...this is a lot stronger than I remember...

Joe walks towards the shifting pile of clothes. As he gets closer, he can smell the sharp mixture of body odor and acrid smoke.

...Is that...

Joe can see the Wheelchair Man laid out on the ground. Joe searches up and down the sidewalk but doesn't see the wheelchair nearby. He gets closer and can hear Wheelchair Man mumbling, half conscious. Joe is stunned. The soft, slow-motion feeling starts to feel like being stuck amber. Joe can't move, and his mind is locked. He feels frozen.

...Call 911...

It feels like forever between the thought and reaching for his phone. A voice on the other end asks for his location. Joe can hear his eyeballs clicking as he blinks.

"Hale. I'm on Hale and Bellaire, I think. Look, there's a guy lying on the sidewalk here, and his wheelchair is missing. He looks like he's in bad shape."

Joe looks down and can see Wheelchair Man's chest rising and falling. Joe takes his overcoat off and throws it down on the man. The voice on the phone sounds miles away.

"Sir! Is the man conscious?"

Joe snaps to attention.

"I'm not sure."

...Not sure this is even real...

Joe bends down and shakes the man's shoulder.

"Yo man, I'm calling for help. They're on the way."

For the first time since Joe walked up, the man moves his body, but only slightly. He turns his chin towards Joe.

"Go fuck yourself."

The voice of the operator crackles from Joe's phone through the night air.

"Sir, we've been out to this location twice already tonight. He's refused any assistance."

"What?"

"This gentleman has refused our help already tonight. Is he conscious?"

Joe collapses on the sidewalk next to the man. Grief rolls over him.

"What are you talking about?"

As he leans over the man's body, Joe can barely hear when the operator says the words right to refuse

"Dude, we need to get you out of the cold."

The man's eye slides upward in Joe's direction. His blue lips tremble.

"Fuck. Off."

"Hello? Sir? I can send someone if he wants help. Sir?"

Joe stares at his phone and ends the call. He turns to the Wheelchair Man.

"Where do you live? I'll take you."

Wheelchair Man pushes the coat off his shoulders and turns his face towards the concrete sidewalk.

Silence.

Panic and despair loop through Joe.

...Nothing makes sense...

For the second time tonight, Joe tells himself it's time to leave Denver.

...Enough bullshit...

8th & Albion

...Can I just press pause...it shouldn't have to be a struggle...can I just have joy...even only for tonight...

Laura stands in the kitchen, molly tab in one hand, bottle of wine in the other.

...All my friends were so at peace tonight...can I have that...

Laura considers the pill in her hand.

...Even if it is a lie...

Laura takes the molly.

...Just a little lift...

Laura watches Nathan and his girls wiggling and giggling on the floor. A bluetooth speaker next to them plays the sound of a woman singing over a repetitive bass heavy drone.

...We all have something weighing us

down...last year almost killed me...and now this stupid mistake with Joe...

Laura sips the wine.

...Just a little joy...

Laura upends the wine bottle.

...Ugh, shut up...

Laura goes into the bedroom and locks the door behind her. She curls up on the bed, pulling the covers around her.

...Life can get better...

...Life will get better...

...Let it go...

...Float...

8th & Albion

Joe wakes up in his bathtub to the sound of someone pissing. It's one of Nathan's girls. She washes her hands and sees Joe peeking out from the shower curtain. She looks at him in the mirror.

"You snore." She closes the door as she leaves the bathroom.

...Get moving...

Joe climbs out of the tub. His muscles are leaden. He unzips his jeans and the splash of his piss against the ceramic bowl is crystalline in his ears.

...Ungh...

He stares balefully at himself in the mirror. He's wearing last night's clothes. His eyes are red and his tongue is fat and furry in his mouth. His whole head feels like a bruise.

...You're still alive...

He opens the cold water tap and lets it run. Joe splashes his face and swishes water around in his mouth.

...Almost like I'm human...

He can hear voices and movement on the other side of the door. He dries his face and hands and walks out into the living room.

...Anybody home...

Joe blinks in the bright morning light streaming from the living room window. There are three silhouettes standing in the living room.

...Where's Laura...

Laura walks out of the bedroom, "We're going to brunch. The car is almost here. You coming?

...We made it to Sunday...

Joe turns to reach for his overcoat from the coat hook by the front door and immediately remembers leaving it on the sidewalk. He grabs his black puffer jacket instead.

...Shit...

Joe locks the door and follows everyone downstairs. They're already in the car; Laura is sitting up front. Joe gets in the back with the two girls in between him and Nathan.

Joe presses his forehead on the cold glass window.

...Am I still high...how much longer will this go on...

The nausea siting in his stomach rises as he thinks about Wheelchair Man freezing on the sidewalk. Laura's words echo in his head about ruining a good time.

Joe pulls out his cell phone and searches the local news for anything about a homeless man dying overnight.

20th & York

The driver pulls the car into the parking lot of the restaurant and the five of them stumble into the late morning sun. Joe watches Laura pull out her phone and finish the ride.

...We all look like shit...except her...somehow...she looks at peace...

They walk in and check in with the host. Her smile fades when she sees Joe dragging ass behind everyone.

"Sorry, we're looking at a 45-minute wait for a table of five."

Joe points out three open tables. The host doesn't look at him while explaining those tables are reserved.

Laura tells the host they'll wait and pulls Joe by his coat sleeve to sit down next to her on the green leather benches that line both sides of the entrance.

"Cut them some slack. When's the last time you broke a sweat for minimum wage?"

Joe ignores Nathan's question and distracts himself by trying to identify the early 80's rock music playing over the speakers. Two young women across from him giggle behind their phones. Joe scowls at them.

A group of seven people walk in, and the host seats them right away.

...Are you fucking kidding me...

They are finally seated, at a dirty table. The waiter brings menus to the table.

"Can we get a wipe down here?"

"No problem, bro."

Laura touches Joe's hand. He looks around and everyone at the table is staring at him. Nathan's girls sit agape in a mixture of horror and glee. Joe looks into Laura's eyes.

...I gotta calm the fuck down...

Nathan reaches across the table and hands Laura two pills, "I've got something to mellow you both out."

Laura looks at them. "Xanies? Thanks, Nathan. what's your handle, I'll drop you some cash."

Laura puts the pills on the table and pulls out her phone. Joe sees the waiter walking over with a towel, and without thinking, he grabs the two pills. Before Laura says anything, Joe gets up and brushes past the waiter to the bathroom.

The bathroom is empty. Joe turns on the water and listens to it run.

...Feels like I'm dissolving...

Joe looks up to see Laura standing behind him in the mirror. Her eyes quickly scan the urinals in the corner and the stall in the other corner. She turns back to Joe.

Before she can say anything, Joe throws the pills in his mouth and scoops water into his mouth from the faucet.

Laura shakes her head, "Do you even know what you just took?"

Joe looks at himself in the mirror. The water is still running.

"I couldn't let you."

"Thank you for caring so much, but I don't need you to save me."

Laura takes Joe's hand and turns to walk out of the bathroom with him.

Joe collapses on the bathroom floor. His breathing stops as everything fades.

Monday, January 3, 2022

12th & Eudora

Laura wakes up in yesterday's clothes. Louanne is at the airport. Laura looks up at the floorboards. The house is quiet.

...Dead...is he really dead...

Laura sits up, searching for a cigarette. She looks around the basement, scans the floor, pats the pocket of the hoodie she's wearing.

...Ugh...I'm still wearing his clothes...

Laura quickly strips and throws the sweats in the corner at the foot of the stairs. She sits down on the foot of the bed, pulling the blanket off, and wraps it around her shoulders.

She picks up the plastic bag of her belongings they gave her when she left the jail. There are no cigarettes in the bag, but she can feel the weight of her phone.

...Let's see...

Laura turns it on. Her notifications start going off immediately.

...Holy shit...

One of the notifications is a link someone sent to a news article headlined "Denver Woman Arrested in Fentanyl Overdose Death". Laura taps her phone. Her eyes scan the article.

"Denver Police reports indicate Davis was arrested after Joseph Price was pronounced dead. While no charges have been filed, investigators have identified Davis as a person of interest."

...It should have been me...what a terrible mistake...what a horrible waste...

The front door opens upstairs, and the sound of her mother's voice filters down through the floor as Laura keeps reading.

"This tragic situation underscores the deadly risks associated with counterfeit pills and fentanyl contamination," stated DPD spokesperson, Erica Ramirez. "Even unintentional distribution can carry devastating consequences."

...No shit, Erica...

Laura throws her phone against the basement wall.

"Laura?"

...Katherine has arrived...pull it together...

Joe died a little more than 30 hours ago. They questioned Laura until Louanne and a lawyer showed up this morning. Laura's mother is back in Denver for the first time since the overdose.

...Here to clean up my mess...again...

The basement door opens and Laura's mother tentatively steps down on the top stair.

"Are you okay, honey?"

"I'm okay, mom."

The air is still after the crackle of her phone shattering and falling to the floor. Laura looks at her mother's hiking sandals.

...How many more times can she come to my rescue...

"The lawyer is going to be here soon. Get dressed, I'll make tea." Laura listens to her mother's steps retreat to the kitchen.

...As long as she draws breath...

The heaviness of Joe's hand in hers as he fell to the floor floods into Laura's mind. She knew right away to check his breathing. She heard nothing and started screaming for help.

...All the stories from rehab should have prepared me...

Joe's lips were blue. His eyes had rolled back and were showing white. She bent down to give him mouth to mouth, but his lifeless face felt stiff and rubbery. Laura recoiled. The memory makes her shiver. She pulls the blanket tighter and her body heaves as if shaken.

Laura inhales deeply, stinging droplets welling in her eyes.

...First, a shower...fresh clothes...some food...

Laura exhales and quietly sobs, face in her hands.

...Deal with the lawyer...say thank you...to everyone...

Laura inhales, swallowing back the flow of tears.

...Get a new phone...maybe...

Laura exhales, stands up, letting the blanket fall from her shoulders.

Laura wipes her eyes, looking up at the fading evening sky through the cellar window.

...Cheers, friend...maybe next time...

Laura inhales...

About the Author

James P. Johnson lives and works in Denver, Colorado. This is the second book in his Burn Sizzle Bleed series.